Olive Oh
Saves Saturday

By Tina Kim • Illustrated by Tiff Bartel

Book design by Sarah Taplin
Illustrations by Tiff Bartel

Published in the United States by Jolly Fish Press, an imprint of North Star Editions, Inc.

First Edition
First Printing, 2021

Library of Congress Cataloging-in-Publication Data (pending)
978-1-63163-571-7 (paperback)
978-1-63163-570-0 (hardcover)

Jolly Fish Press
North Star Editions, Inc.
2297 Waters Drive
Mendota Heights, MN 55120
www.jollyfishpress.com

Printed in the United States of America

Table of Contents

ALL ABOUT OLIVE OH 5

CHAPTER 1 9

CHAPTER 2 17

CHAPTER 3 24

CHAPTER 4 37

CHAPTER 5 45

CHAPTER 6 52

CHAPTER 7 61

CHAPTER 8 76

CHAPTER 9 88

CHAPTER 10 102

All About
Olive Oh

Hi! I'm Olive Sun-Hee Oh. I live in Los Angeles, California. Right now I'm in third grade, but I am going to be a professional artist one day.

Here are some of the most important facts about me:

- I got my middle name, Sun-Hee, from my grandma. She's an amazing knitter, and she makes me the coolest hats.

- My mom, Julie, works as an interior designer, which is like being an artist for people's homes.

- My brother, Ray, is in sixth grade. He loves K-pop and is a pretty good dancer.

- My sister, Shelly, is in ninth grade. She's going to be a doctor one day, like our dad was.

- My dad died before my first birthday. I don't remember him since I was so little, but Shelly and Ray tell me he was the best dad ever. We keep a photo of him by the door so we can wave hello and goodbye as we come and go.

- My best friend, Marcus Wong, is the bestest friend you could ever have. We've known each other since kindergarten. That's a long time!

Other fun facts about me:

- I love the color red because it's so bright and pretty. And green, because it makes me feel calm. And blue, because it reminds me of the ocean. Also yellow, orange, and purple—I love purple! You've probably guessed it by now: I have a LOT of favorite colors.

- My favorite food is sujebi soup. It's my grandma's specialty because it's made with lots of Halmoni Sarang. (That means "Grandma Love.")

- What's the most interesting thing about me? My freckles! My freckles are special because they look like a constellation. On my nose, you can find the Big Dipper, which is a pattern of stars that look like a ladle. Pretty cool, huh?

Chapter 1

I, Olive Sun-Hee Oh, am a girl who loves adventure. What kind of adventure, you ask? Things like climbing the big tree in our backyard or racing my older brother Ray down the street on our bikes.

And in exactly six days, I will be going on the adventure of a lifetime. My best friend Marcus Wong and his parents are going camping, and they're taking me with them! Greta and Cory, my friends from school, are coming too. Ever since our school's art show, Marcus and I have been hanging out with Greta and

Cory a lot more. We have lots of fun because they both love art like I do.

Next weekend, we will be camping under the stars at Big Bear Lake. I've never been there before, but I know that at night, I'll be able to see all kinds of constellations. And I'll be able to show my friends all the cool stuff I know about them.

Here in Los Angeles, the very best place to see constellations is at the Griffith Observatory using a telescope. But out in the wilderness, you can just look up at the sky. While we're camping, I want to see as many stars as possible.

Which is why I can't clean my room today—I lost

my *Handbook of Constellations*, and I need that for the camping trip. Nothing is as important as looking for my handbook. Definitely not cleaning my room!

Besides, it's really not that messy. Most of my clothes are put away. Except for a few T-shirts. And some clothes from my closet, but I had to move those to look for my book. It took me all morning to pull them all out, but the book wasn't there. Now I'm looking under my bed. I see a few socks, my red beret that Grandma knitted for me, and my polka-dot overalls. But no handbook.

Next, I look under my blanket. I spot a book with a blue cover, so I grab it fast. But when I look at it closely, it's just my art sketchbook. Still no handbook. It's time to call for backup.

I poke my head out my door and yell, "Mom!"

Seconds later, I hear footsteps coming down the hall. It's Ray with his headphones on. He's been listening to the same K-pop song over and over again. His dance group has a competition coming up, so Ray has been practicing the routine in his room. Sometimes he's in there for hours! Ray says he loves dancing more than I love art, but I disagree. I love art *way* more than he loves dancing.

"Whoa," Ray says, taking his headphones off. He

looks inside my bedroom. "You are so in trouble when Mom sees your room."

"No, I'm not. Go away!" My brother thinks that because he is in middle school, he knows everything and can boss me around. But that's not true. Or fair.

Ray leaves just as Mom comes to my room, but he turns around to say, "Mom, check out Olive's room."

"Hey!" I yell at my brother.

I want to yell some more, but Mom asks, "What's wrong, Olive?"

"Nothing! Don't listen to Ray." I give Mom a sweet smile. "Have you seen my *Handbook of Constellations*?"

Mom puts her hands on her sides. Uh-oh. That is not a good sign.

"Olive, did you call for me because you lost a book?"

"Not just any book. My *Handbook of Constellations*. I need it for the camping trip."

Mom doesn't answer me. Instead, she steps inside my room and takes a look around.

"Olive," Mom says. "Why is your room so messy? Today is cleaning day."

Oops.

"I know, but I can't find my handbook," I say.

Mom takes a deep breath. "Maybe if you clean your

room, you will find the book. It could be under one of your hats."

Hmm. Mom does have a point. The handbook is small enough to be hiding under my clothes. Now that Mom mentions it, I see that *most* of my clothes are on my bedroom floor.

"Okay, Mom. I'll clean up," I say with a smile. "I promise."

Mom finally smiles too. "And I'll keep an eye out for your book."

"Thanks, Mom."

My mom is the bestest and smartest mom. Do you

want to know why? Because as soon as I picked up all my clothes from the floor, guess what I found?

The *Handbook of Constellations*! Right underneath my orange tie-dye shirt.

Now I'm ready for the camping trip.

Chapter 2

On Monday, I get to class extra early so I can tell Marcus that I found my handbook. Our camping adventure would have been a disaster without it.

"Good morning, Olive," Marcus says when I get to my seat.

I wave hello. "Marcus, guess what? I saved our camping trip."

"What do you mean?" he asks.

I open up my backpack and take out the book. "Ta-da! I'd thought I lost this, but I found it while cleaning my room. Now we don't have to worry about missing any stars."

Marcus takes a look at it. "Cool. My dad is going to pack some binoculars for us. With your book, I bet we'll find lots of constellations."

"Awesome," I say. Marcus's dad loves stars like I do. In fact, when the Wongs got their cat, they named her Cassiopeia, like the constellation in the northern sky.

Just then, Mrs. Bramble walks in. "Good morning, class. Did you all have a nice weekend?"

"Yes, Mrs. Bramble!" we all say. A few students look a little sleepy. One is my friend Cory. He is not a morning person. In fact, his hair is smooshed down on one side, like he just rolled out of bed. I'm not usually a morning person either, but today I was so excited about the camping trip that I woke up bright and early. I'm already imagining all the fun things we're going to do up in the mountains. The air will be crisp and clean. Creatures will be hooting and chirping, and the stars will be shining.

Or at least that's what Grandma told me last night. She said that when my dad was a little boy, she and my grandpa used to take him camping. Grandma would pack a picnic of kimbap and instant ramen, and Grandpa would bring his fishing gear. They would spend the day exploring nature. Then at night, they would camp under the stars. She said this was one of her favorite things to do as a family.

I stop daydreaming when I realize Mrs. Bramble has started talking about science. This week, we're learning about plants and the environments where they grow. Today, Mrs. Bramble tells us how some plants grow in really dry places.

"Certain plants, such as the cactus or aloe vera, not only survive but thrive in harsh climates," she says. "These desert plants have a thick exterior that shields them from the heat while holding water inside."

"Wow," I whisper to Marcus, who nods.

"Scientists learned this by writing down their

observations about different plant species. Today, we will be doing the same."

Mrs. Bramble places a box on top of her desk and takes out several photos of different kinds of flowers.

"I want each of you to pick out a photo of a flower and draw it with as much detail as you can in your notebook. Then, write down what you see. What color is your flower? Does it have any special features that stand out? And do you think this plant would grow better in an environment that is dry or wet?"

Drawing for school? What a cool assignment!

Marcus and I go to the front of the classroom and each pick out a photo. I choose a purple-blue flower with small white dots on the petals. I hold it up to show Marcus. "This flower has freckles like I do!" I say, and we both laugh.

"What did you pick?" I ask him. He holds up a photo of a strange flower that looks like a long, sharp beak.

"How cool," I say. When we get back to our seats, I imagine that I'm a scientist wearing a lab coat and goggles. I feel ready to make an important discovery. I open up my notebook and start drawing.

I'm already an artist, so this part is easy. First, I make a quick sketch. Next, I color it in with the colored pencils I keep in my backpack. Then, I move on to the questions. While I'm writing the answers, I get a great idea. I can take my notebook on the camping trip this weekend and write down observations of all the plants I find in the mountains. It'll be amazing.

Observations
1. Colors: dark purple-blue and white
2. special features: freckles on the petals
3. climate: probably a wet climate because the leaves and petals are thin

Chapter 3

When Ray, Shelly, and I get home after school, Grandma is in the kitchen cooking. My grandma is always busy, either knitting or making something delicious. She's a creative person, and I'm just like her, probably because we share the same name.

Yesterday, Grandma started making a hat for me to take on my camping trip. She knits most of my hats, but this time she used a sewing machine to make a big, floppy hat to protect me from the sun. It's bright blue, which happens to be one of my favorite colors.

Today, she's been cooking something that makes the whole house smell amazing.

"Halmoni, what smells so good?" I run to her, but my grandma is already wheeling toward me. We meet halfway in the living room for a bear hug. My grandma's bear hugs are the best.

She laughs. "I made pajeon for everybody."

"Yum," my sister Shelly says. She and Ray are still taking their shoes off by the front door. Mom is right behind them.

I hurry into the kitchen with Grandma for a taste test. Pajeon is a savory Korean pancake with green onions. The best part is that you get to dip each bite in soy sauce to make it even yummier. Also, green onions are vegetables, so pajeon counts as a healthy snack. At least, I think it should. But Mom doesn't agree.

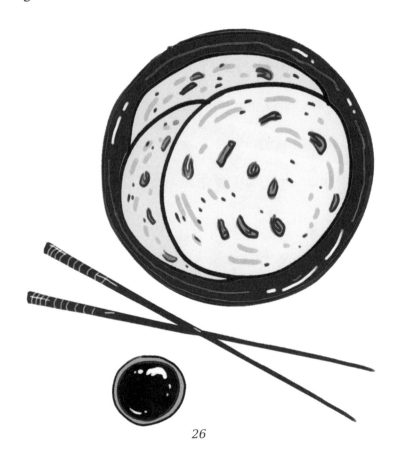

Ray goes to sit at the dining table. "It smells so good."

Shelly and Mom join him. I help my grandma take the plates to the table and give everyone chopsticks.

"Olive, you are so helpful today," Mom says.

"Yeah," Ray says. "You never help out unless Mom tells you to."

"I'm always helpful," I say. Then I stick my tongue out at my brother. Lucky for me, Mom doesn't see it.

"Is this because you got in trouble for your messy room?" Shelly asks.

"No!"

"Yes, it is," Ray says. "Your room was messier than mine."

"Olive," Shelly begins, "you have to be more organized. And so do you, Ray."

"Hey!" Ray says, but he is smirking at me. "At least I'm not as bad as Olive."

"True," Shelly says, "though that's still far from clean."

My cheeks feel hot, like I'm in one of those desert climates Mrs. Bramble was talking about today. Why are Shelly and Ray being so mean? It's not fair when they team up on me like this.

"Shelly and Ray, leave your sister alone," Mom says.

"Yeah!" I shout.

"Olive." Mom gives me a warning look. I quickly close my mouth, but in my head, I am still yelling at my brother and sister.

Grandma comes over and gives me a kiss on the cheek. It makes me a little less mad. At least *someone* likes me.

"Thanks, Halmoni," I say to her. My cheeks cool down a little. But I'm still mad at Shelly and Ray.

After we're done eating, I go to my room and shut the door. Sometimes I need time alone because having siblings can take up a *lot* of energy. Especially when you have older siblings who always pick on you. They just don't understand that my bedroom is also my art studio, so of course it's messy. One day, when I'm a professional artist, my studio will be as messy as I want it to be. And it will be awesome!

But I will admit that every once in a while, it can be helpful to be organized. For instance, I do need to organize some ideas for the camping trip. Shelly taught me that making lists is a good way to get your ideas organized, so I guess having older siblings can be helpful too. Sometimes.

I grab a notebook from my backpack and start a list of all the things I'll need to pack for this weekend.

I've never been on a trip without my family. And it couldn't have come at a more perfect time. I get two whole days without Shelly and Ray bugging me!

I look around my bedroom. What do I need?

Mrs. Wong said we would need to wear layers, so I decide to start with clothes.

I open my closet. My clothes are so colorful—so *me*. I love them all, so which ones should I bring? Suddenly, I know: my artist's smock. Originally, it was an old apron Mom was going to throw away, but I kept it to wear when I'm making art, which is often very messy. There are many *layers* of paint smudges. Also, it has two pockets on the front. I can put both my notebook and my handbook in them. Perfect!

I grab my pencil to add more items to the list:

- Slime (for the car ride)
- Puzzles of cats (in case we get bored)
- A lasso I won at the county fair (could be useful, who knows?)
- Lots of banana milk for sharing
- Cups of instant ramen (just like Grandma packed for her family trips with Dad)
- Glow-in-the-dark stars (in case of an emergency)
- All of my art supplies, including my new paint set

I'm gathering my supplies when I hear a knock on my door.

"Come in!" I shout.

Mom pokes her head in. She looks around my room. Uh-oh. Not again.

"Olive . . ."

"Mom, I've got everything under control," I say. "When I'm done packing, my room will be squeaky-clean."

"I hope so." Mom comes in and sits on my bed. She looks at my slime. "Are you taking this too?"

"It's not a camping trip without slime, Umma," I

say. I pick up the lime-green slime and mold it into a ball in my hand. *Squishhh.* It's so much fun!

"All right. Just make sure you take a warm jacket. Nighttime is chilly up there," she says.

"A jacket!" I exclaim. "That's what I forgot."

"There's also a flashlight in the garage," Mom says. "And some sunscreen too."

"Okay, but nothing else. I don't have enough room," I say.

Mom picks up my box of crayons. "Maybe you can take the twelve-pack instead?"

I groan. "But I need all one hundred eighty colors."

"Just think about it, okay?" Mom asks me.

"Okay."

"The house will be very quiet this weekend without you, Shelly, and Ray," Mom says.

Ray has that K-pop dance competition at the Korean Music Festival at St. Andrews Park. He and his friends have been practicing for weeks. It's their first time competing against other dance groups, which means Ray won't stop talking about it. There will be a big stage set up in the park so the audience can watch the performances.

Mom and Grandma are going to take a picnic and make a day out of it. They'll cheer extra loud since Shelly and I can't go.

I'll be camping, and my sister is going on a field trip to some fancy garden to hear a very important speaker talk about college. She's super excited because the event is all about school and studying. It sounds pretty boring to me. What's the point of being outdoors if all you do is sit and listen to someone talk? I'd rather be out exploring—and I will be! Of all the plans for this weekend, I think mine is definitely the best.

Chapter 4

On Wednesday, Marcus, Greta, Cory, and I have a Very Important Planning Meeting in the cafeteria during lunch. We take our trays of Mac-and-Cheese Surprise to an empty table.

"What do you think is the surprise?" Cory asks, eyeing his food suspiciously.

Marcus pokes at his meal with his fork. Greta ties back her curly hair, unfolds her napkin, and lays it out on her lap as if she is preparing for a messy meal.

"I'll take a sniff," I offer, putting my nose closer to my tray. My friends watch me.

"Well?" Greta asks. "What does it smell like?"

"Does it smell good?" Marcus asks.

"It's some kind of meat," I say. The smell is familiar, sort of like hamburger, but not quite. I'll need to investigate more, like a scientist. I take another sniff, and this time my nose tells me.

"It's sausage!" I say.

"Yeah!" Greta and Cory shout at the same time.

Marcus and I high-five.

"It's pasta and hot dogs rolled into one," Marcus says. "Genius!"

We gobble up our lunch, but Greta looks a little down.

"Greta, what's wrong?" I ask. "Is something wrong with your Mac-and-Cheese Surprise?"

Greta shakes her head. "I have some bad news. I can't go on the camping trip anymore."

"What?!" Marcus, Cory, and I yell.

"You have to come! We were going to have so much fun together," I say.

"I know," Greta says. "But my mom changed her mind. I've never gone on a trip without my parents. They said maybe next year."

"Oh, man," Cory mutters.

After that, no one says anything for a while. I don't even want to finish the rest of my lunch because I'm so sad.

"You guys can still have fun without me," Greta says. "Sorry I ruined the trip."

"You didn't ruin the trip, Greta," Marcus says. "We'll just make sure to go again next year so you can come."

Greta perks up. "You bet!"

I'm glad Marcus can say nice things at a time like this. It would be very hard for me to do that. It was going to be a great adventure. Now, without Greta, the camping trip won't be so great.

When Mom picks me up after school, I tell her about Greta not being able to go camping. After I'm done, I let out a sad sigh. Outside the car window, the sky looks dark gray with big clouds. It's gloomy, just like my mood.

"Honey, I'm sure you'll still have lots of fun," Mom says.

"I know, but I was going to show Greta the constellations."

"I'm sorry, sweetheart," Mom says. "You can still show Marcus and Cory. I have an idea. Why don't we go to the Korean market and buy snacks to share with them?"

"Really? Okay!"

When we get to the store, I leave Mom with the vegetables and fruits and run to my favorite aisle: snacks.

I look at the chips and crackers first. I grab a pink bag of sweet-potato chips. It's the best snack to eat anytime *or* anywhere. Next to it, there is a bag of onion rings. Yum! Another great choice for camping. In fact, choosing camping snacks is not an easy task. There are so many delicious options.

A while later, when I've finally moved on to the candy section, Mom finds me.

"Olive," Mom says. "Are all of those the snacks you picked out?"

I look down at the snacks I chose. They're dumped in a pile on the floor next to me.

I smile at my mom very sweetly. "Yes, Umma."

Mom shakes her head, but she is smiling. "Please put them in the cart. Let's go pay for these now before you add anything else."

"Thanks, Mom," I say. "And I think you're right. I can still have a great camping trip."

Chapter 5

Pitter-patter. Pitter-patter.

This sound wakes me up on Friday morning.

I open my eyes and jump out of bed. I run to the window and open up the blinds. Outside, everything is wet. It's raining!

"Mom!" I yell, rushing out of my bedroom and into hers. She is just getting up. Ray rushes in right behind me.

"I was here first!" I shout at him. My brother folds his arms over his chest, but he lets me talk to Mom first.

"Mom," I yell again. "It's raining! My camping trip is ruined!"

"No," Ray interrupts. "You can just go later. But if the rain ruins my competition—"

"No one cares about your competition!" I yell at my brother.

"Ray. Olive. Please," Mom says in her groggy voice. "Give me a minute to wake up."

She stands up slowly and yawns. Then she looks out her window. "Let's check the weather report. Maybe it's a passing rain."

Mom goes to the living room. Ray and I follow close behind.

Grandma and Shelly are at the kitchen counter. They are drinking tea.

"Good morning," Grandma says.

"Good morning, Grandma," Ray and I mutter as Mom turns on the TV. I hold my breath as she finds the weather channel. Right on cue, a reporter comes on the screen.

"Wet weather is headed to the southland all day, so pack your umbrellas," she says. "But not to worry, the rain should let up by tomorrow morning for a sunny California weekend."

"Phew!" Ray says, and I stop holding my breath.

We both fall back on the couch. Thank goodness the rain will be gone by tomorrow.

For today though, Mom tells me I have to wear my rain boots. I do not like rain boots. They are the worst kind of shoes. Did you know rain boots are terrible for running? And they're even worse for climbing trees. They're too big and clunky. Definitely not good shoes for an adventurer like me.

"Would you rather have soggy socks?" Shelly asks me on her way out to the school bus. As always, she is very prepared. She has a raincoat, rain boots, *and* an umbrella.

I want to ignore her, but then I imagine my feet

going *squish, squish* in my shoes all day long. It would feel like my shoes were filled with slime. Yuck. Usually I love slime, but I don't want it in my shoes.

"Eww, no!" I exclaim. I hurry to put my feet into my rain boots.

By the time Mom drops me off at school, the rain is barely a sprinkle. Maybe it will stop before the end of the day.

Outside the schoolyard, I see some of my classmates in a circle with one person in the middle. It's Ally, a girl in my class who is a jazz dancer. She is leaping into puddles and showing off her dance moves.

"She's so good," Greta says. She tries to do a spin

like Ally but nearly falls. Luckily, Greta plants her foot down to stop herself. She makes a big splash in a puddle of water.

"Hey, that looks fun," I say. I stomp a foot. *Splash*. Then I jump up and down. I make a bigger splash. Greta joins. Every time we make a splash, water gets all over our boots, but our clothes are still dry.

"This *is* fun!" I exclaim. I like jumping in puddles. As long as the rain goes away by tomorrow, I might even *love* puddles.

Chapter 6

Later that morning, Mrs. Bramble continues her lesson on plants and flowers.

"Some plant species can grow in many different environments," she starts. "That is due to their ability to adapt, which means they can change and grow to match their environment. Orchids are one example."

From under her desk, Mrs. Bramble pulls out several potted plants. Each one has beautiful flowers. "All these plants are orchids," she explains. "Aren't they lovely? They come in many colors and shapes, but they are all from the same family. Isn't it wonderful that they can be so different yet still belong to one family?"

Everybody nods, but I think about my family. It's not always so wonderful with me and my siblings. We are *too* different.

"There are many types of orchids," Mrs. Bramble goes on. "Each one has adapted to live in a different place. I love orchids because they remind me that even in tough situations, we can grow and flourish."

"I didn't know flowers could be so interesting," Marcus says. I'm about to agree when I hear a sound outside.

Pitter-patter. Pitter-patter. Pitter-patter.

The rain has started up again. It's much faster and louder than it was earlier.

I turn to Marcus. "I really hope this rain is gone by tomorrow."

"Me too," he says.

Marcus and I look out the window. Rain pours from the dark clouds. The whole sky is gray. That is not a good sign. We both cross our fingers for luck, because we really need it.

After school that day, Shelly, Ray, and I are sitting on the couch watching TV. I keep looking out the window because the rain is still pouring.

Grandma is sitting in front of the window. Usually, she knits and watches our street for cars and people taking walks, but today she is just listening to the rain. I don't need to sit near the window to do that—the rain is so loud I can hear it just fine from the couch.

Next to me, Ray is very sulky. The Korean Music Festival got postponed because of the rain, which means no dance competition.

"Can't they move the competition indoors?" Shelly asks him.

"It's too last-minute to find a place," Ray says. "All that practice for nothing."

"You'll have other competitions, Ray," my sister says. "It's not like this will affect your grades or anything."

As soon as she says that, Ray jumps up off the couch. "All you ever think about is school!" he yells and stomps off to his room.

"Hey!" Shelly yells after him, but he slams the door.

I look at my sister.

"I'll talk to him after he's calmed down," she tells me. I nod. I'm glad that she is the older sister and not me. Ray looked *very* mad. I guess I'd be mad too if something important to me got cancelled. Something like my camping trip.

I go back to staring out the window and worrying about my trip until I see the headlights from Mom's car. She went to get some pizza for dinner to help cheer us up.

"Pizza is here!" I yell extra loud so Ray can hear. Maybe that will help him feel better.

"Olive, help me set the table," Shelly says.

"Okay," I answer, but only because the sooner we set the table, the sooner we can eat.

While my sister and I are in the kitchen, I hear Mom come inside. She's talking to someone on her phone.

"Yes, I understand," she is saying. "I know. It's too bad, but what can you do?"

By the time the table is set, Mom hangs up the phone.

"Who was that?" Grandma asks.

Mom has a frown on her face. She looks straight at me.

Suddenly, I get a sinking feeling in the pit of my stomach.

"Olive, I'm so sorry . . ." Mom starts.

I hold my breath and hope she's not going to say what I think she's going to say. But she does.

"The camping trip is cancelled."

"No!" I yell.

Before Mom can say anything else, I run to my

room and slam my door. I stay in my room for the rest of the night. I don't even eat the pizza Grandma brings me.

My great camping adventure is ruined.

Chapter 7

This is the worst Saturday morning *ever*. My camping trip is ruined. Ray's dance competition isn't happening. Even Shelly's trip to the fancy garden is cancelled. All because of this horrible rain. I'm in such a bad mood that I just want to stay in bed all day.

A few minutes ago, Mom asked me, Shelly, and Ray to get up for breakfast, but we are *all* in a bad mood. Shelly won't even read a book. Usually books make her feel better, but the rain is ruining even her favorite thing.

"Olive?" I hear at my door. It's Grandma. "Can I come in?" she asks.

Even though I don't want to see anybody, I can't say no to Grandma.

"Okay." I sit up in my bed as she comes inside.

"I know today is a difficult day for you, but your mom is making pancakes," she says.

Normally I love pancakes, but today is the worst Saturday ever, so I tell her I'm not hungry. Then my stomach growls so loud it sounds like an angry cat.

Oops. I guess I am a little hungry. I look at Grandma, but she doesn't seem to have heard it.

"You can come back to your room right after breakfast," Grandma says. "What do you say?"

Maybe I'll have one pancake and then come back to bed. I won't even enjoy it (that much).

"Okay, Halmoni," I say. "I'll have breakfast."

When I walk into the kitchen, Mom says, "Thank you for joining us, Olive."

Ray and Shelly are already sitting at the table. They have big frowns on their faces.

"Mom, can we have our pancakes now?" Shelly asks. "I'd like to hurry up and eat so I can go back to my room."

"What are you so upset about?" Ray asks as Mom

gives each of us a pancake. "It was just a field trip to hear someone talk about school."

Shelly's frown gets bigger. "School is important. Not like a dance competition."

"Yeah," I agree.

Ray turns to me. "At least it's more important than camping."

"No, it's not!" I say.

Shelly crosses her arms. "None of those are as important as going to college, okay?"

Ray and I both talk over each other, telling Shelly that she is wrong. Actually, they are *both* wrong. Camping is the adventure of a lifetime. Seeing the stars is *way* cooler than dancing or listening to some boring grown-up talk. I'm extra mad I'm not camping right now because if I were, I wouldn't be stuck in the house with my brother and sister.

Mom sighs very loudly. She is looking down at her plate of pancakes, but she's not eating them. Shelly, Ray, and I all stop talking. Uh-oh. Usually it's just two of us fighting, but today it's all three of us. We can't help that we're so different. Still, Mom looks very upset.

"Everyone," Mom begins, "please try to understand one another. I know you are all disappointed, but you don't need to get angry at each other. Can you please apologize?"

We all murmur "sorry" to each other.

"Thank you," Mom says. "Since everybody's plans didn't work out, how about we take a family trip to the art museum?"

Ray and I look at Shelly. She usually jumps at the chance to go to a museum, but today she shakes her head no. Ray and I shake our heads too. Even art won't cheer me up today.

Then Grandma says, "There is a new Korean drama on TV this morning. Who wants to watch with me?"

I wouldn't mind watching TV, but Shelly and Ray are shaking their heads, so I shake my head too. Mom sighs again. She is starting to look grumpy just like us. But instead of saying anything, she gives each of us another pancake. I'm secretly glad because Mom makes great pancakes.

Just as I'm eating the last bite, Mom's phone rings. She answers it and looks at me.

"Olive, it's Marcus. He'd like to talk to you," she says.

"Okay," I say. "Can I take it in my room? I'd like some privacy."

I heard Shelly say this once, and it sounded really grown-up. Now, when I say it, she rolls her eyes. But Shelly isn't the only one who gets important phone calls. I do too!

"Yes, you may," Mom says.

"Thank you." I take the phone and go to my room. Of course, I close the door.

"Hello?" I say into the phone.

"Hey, Olive. It's Marcus." Hearing my best friend's voice makes me even sadder that we're not camping together.

"Olive?" Marcus asks. "How are you?"

I tell him the truth. "I'm not having a very fun Saturday. How about you?"

"I'm really upset about the trip," he says. "I didn't even want to get out of bed this morning."

"Me either!" I say. "But I had to get up because my mom made pancakes."

Marcus laughs. "You can't say no to pancakes!"

"No, you can't." I laugh too. "I feel a little better talking to you, Marcus."

"Me too," he says. The coolest thing about having a BFF is that they are always on the same page as you and they understand exactly how you feel—unlike your siblings.

"What are you going to do today?" I ask him.

"Well, I was thinking about the assignment we had in class about observing flowers, and I thought I could do that at home. Mom bought some new plants, and they look really cool. I think one of them might be an orchid."

"That's a great idea," I say.

"I would invite you over, but Mom wants us to have a family day today."

"That's okay." We say goodbye after Marcus promises to show me his notebook of observations when I see him at school.

Even though Marcus is an only child, he doesn't seem to get as lonely as I do. Maybe that's because he has Cassie, his cat. I have a brother *and* a sister, but they never want to hang out with me. Especially not today.

By the time I'm done talking to Marcus, Shelly and Ray are back in their rooms with their doors shut. So I go sit on the living room couch and turn on the TV.

Grandma is in her spot by the window. Mom comes into the room with a laundry basket.

"Olive, would you like to help me fold the laundry?" Mom sits next to me on the couch, dropping the basket on the floor in front of us.

"Do I have to?" I ask.

Mom thinks about it. "No. If you don't want to, you don't have to."

"Okay." I go back to flipping through the channels. I watch Mom fold our clothes and towels by herself. There is a *lot* of laundry.

"Actually, I'd like to help," I say.

Mom gives me a hug. "Thank you. I'll bring the other load."

"There's more?!" I shout.

Grandma chuckles. "Olive, look outside for a little bit. It will make folding laundry more fun."

"It's dark and rainy outside, Halmoni." I can't believe it's still so gloomy.

"But you can imagine that it's sunny. When I was a little girl living in Korea, I used to play make-believe games when it snowed," Grandma tells me.

"It snows in Korea?" I am amazed. It never snows in LA.

"Oh, yes. Winters were very long and cold. I didn't

like that at all, so I pretended that I was somewhere else. Sometimes, I chose a tropical island like Hawaii. Or a city like Paris, France." Grandma stares out the window at the rain. She smiles as if she can see Paris outside instead of our yard.

"But it wasn't real," I tell her.

"True," Grandma replies. "But it made me feel better."

Mom comes back with another basket. This one is filled with blankets and sheets.

"My blanket!" I grab my blue-and-white blanket and wrap it around me like a burrito. It's still warm from the dryer, and it smells so good.

I help Mom finish folding the rest of the laundry with just my arms poking out of my burrito blanket. When we're done, I lie down on the couch and cover myself with the blanket like a tent so I don't have to hear the rain anymore. I close my eyes and think about Grandma's make-believe game. If I could imagine any place I'd rather be, where would I pick?

I don't think I'd like to go to a tropical island. Too much water. Right now, I am *not* a fan of water.

Paris is a great idea. I keep my eyes closed and imagine walking to the Eiffel Tower wearing my red beret. I look very French. Suddenly, my imagination takes me somewhere else. I see mountains and trees and a night sky with no clouds.

When I open my eyes, I'm back in our living room under my blanket. But I know *exactly* where I'd like to be today. And I think I can make that happen.

Chapter 8

"Mom, can I borrow something?" I use my soft, sweet, inside voice that Mom really likes because she says I sound like an angel. That's how I want to sound because I really, really need her to say yes.

"If you borrow it, will I get it back in the same condition?"

"Of course, Umma! I promise."

Last month, I borrowed Mom's special bag made out of straw because I wanted to see if Cassie would fit in it. I saw our neighbor, Mr. Garcia, carrying his new puppy that way. It looked so cute. The puppy's head poked out like it was a little baby. But I think cats are different than puppies, because when I dropped Cassie in the bag, she scratched at it until the bag was shredded into pieces. Mom was *not* happy with me.

"I really, really promise," I repeat.

"Okay, I'm trusting you," Mom says. "What would you like to borrow?"

"All the blankets and sheets," I tell her.

Mom's mouth drops open. "You mean the ones I just washed?"

I nod my head. "It's for something important."

"I don't know, Olive," she says.

"Please, Umma? This will cheer everybody up. I have a plan to save this rainy day!"

"All right," Mom says. "You may use them."

"Yes!" I yell.

Mom's hands fly up to her ears. Oops. I forgot to keep my voice quiet. I can't help it—I'm so excited about my great plan.

I hug Mom to thank her. Then I go into my room to grab my bag of camping supplies. Just as I start to leave, I notice a blue object on my bed. My hat! Grandma must have finished it. I put it on and rush back to the living room.

There, I count five blankets and five sheets. I pile

them in front of the TV. Then I bring in all the chairs from the dining table.

Grandma turns around to get a good look at what I'm doing. "Olive, what are you making?"

"I'm bringing the great outdoors *indoors*," I proclaim. "We are going to camp inside our house!"

"That's a great idea," Grandma says. "And your hat looks wonderful."

I give Grandma a big thumbs-up. "Thank you, Halmoni. I love it!"

"Is there anything I can do to help?" Grandma asks.

I shake my head. "I got this. But can I borrow some safety pins?"

She nods. "You know where to find them."

I run to her room and find her sewing kit. I take out a box of safety pins. I use them to connect the five sheets together so I have one giant sheet. Then, I tie part of this big sheet to the top of each chair. After that, I push the chairs out toward the corners of the room until the sheet is spread out flat.

It looks great, except that the middle of the sheet is falling in. I need something to lift up the middle so it will look like a tent. But what could I use?

Maybe my brother and sister can help.

I run down the hall to Shelly's room and knock on her door. Before she can answer, I knock on Ray's door too. They both poke their heads out of their rooms at the same time.

"What is it, Olive?" Shelly asks. She looks like she has been sleeping. Ray does too.

"I have a surprise for both of you," I say.

"Not now, Olive," Ray says.

"Sorry, Olive. I just want to stay in my room," Shelly adds. She's about to close the door, but I stop her by sticking my foot out.

"Wait! I need help from both of you. This is important."

My brother and sister both sigh.

"Come on," I say. "It will make you feel better." I grab their hands and pull them into the living room.

Shelly and Ray groan. I pretend I don't hear them, like when Mom pretends she doesn't hear me complain about eating Brussels sprouts. (Yuck.)

When we get to the living room, I yell, "TA-DA!"

Shelly and Ray look at the tent that I made with our sheets and chairs. "What is it?" Ray asks.

"It's our tent!" I say. "I made a family camping trip in our living room."

"Olive, this is really nice," Shelly says. "But I don't really want to play."

"Yeah," Ray agrees. "Besides, it doesn't even look

like a tent. See how it flops down in the middle?" He points at the spot where the sheets sag.

"That's what I need help with," I say.

"Hmm." Ray scratches his chin. Next to him, Shelly puts a hand on her hip. They are both thinking, which means they are going to help me!

"If you had a rope, you could lift up the sheet and tie it to the ceiling fan," Ray says.

"A rope?" I ask. Then I remember: my lasso! I open up my bag of camping supplies and take it out. "Will this work?" I ask Ray.

He looks at it. "Sure. I think if you untie it, it will be long enough."

I try to untie it like he suggested, but the knot won't budge. "It's stuck," I tell him. "Can you help?"

Ray still doesn't look very excited, but he nods as he grabs the lasso from me. "Just this, and then I'm going to my room. Shelly, could you help too?"

Shelly sighs, but she doesn't leave. After Ray unties the lasso, she takes one end of the rope. She pulls it underneath the big sheet while Ray holds on to the other end. They bring each end of the rope together to tie around the ceiling fan. I watch as the rope lifts the sheet up high. It looks like a real tent—but bigger and better! I finish up by spreading the blankets under the sheet to make the tent's floor.

We all take a step back to look at the finished product.

"This looks good," I say.

Ray and Shelly nod their heads.

"Something is missing though," I say.

"What?" Ray asks.

"I know," Shelly says. "I'll be right back." My sister runs through our house, going from room to room and grabbing pillows. She even throws a few pillows at me and Ray. We both catch them and laugh.

"What do we do with them?" Ray asks.

"Put them inside, of course," Shelly tells us.

We each take the pillows and tuck them inside the

tent. When we're done, Shelly, Ray, and I lie down. The pillows make a soft, fluffy floor.

"Hey, this is pretty cool," Ray says.

"I guess it's kind of cozy," Shelly admits.

I knew my idea would be a success! And I'm so happy my brother and sister like it.

I clear my throat and declare, "Welcome to the Oh Family Camping Adventure!"

Chapter 9

It's dark outside. I can hear the wind howling, but the sound of the rain isn't as loud as it was in the morning. In fact, it sounds okay. Maybe I got used to it?

After I announced the start of the Oh Family Camping Adventure, we changed into the perfect clothes for indoor camping: pajamas. But I'm keeping my blue hat on because Grandma made it for me and I love it.

"Dinner is ready," Mom says. She brings a large tray to our tent and sets it down so it looks like a mini-table.

In the middle of the tray is a big plate of kimbap. Mom even put Spam inside the seaweed-wrapped rice to make it extra yummy.

"It's like what Grandma ate with Dad and Grandpa on their camping trips," I say.

"Yes," Mom says. "Too bad we're out of ramen. That would have been the perfect combination."

"We're not out!" I say. I grab my bag of supplies and pull out the cups of ramen.

"Way to go, Olive," Shelly says. "You were very prepared for your camping trip."

"Yeah," Ray agrees. "I'm sorry it got cancelled. It seems like it would have been a lot of fun."

Hearing my brother say that makes me feel like being nice, so I say, "I'm sorry your competition got cancelled. You would've been awesome."

Ray tries to smile, but I think he's still sad about it. "This isn't so bad."

Mom gives his shoulder a squeeze. "That's the spirit. I'm sure you'll get on that stage sooner than you think."

"That gives me an idea," I say. "What if you did your performance after dinner? We can be your audience!"

"Yes, Ray," Shelly agrees. "I would love to see your dance moves."

"Okay," Ray says, "but let's eat first."

"Good plan," Mom says. "Let's get these ready."

While Mom goes back into the kitchen to make the ramen, we bring the kimbap to the dining table. Ramen is served steaming hot. Mom said we should eat at a real table so we don't worry about spilling it. But we have to stand because we're using the chairs for our tent!

Mom sets the pot of hot soup in the middle of the table. Shelly, Ray, and I lean our heads in closer, being careful not to touch it. We breathe in the delicious smell. "Perfecto!" Ray exclaims.

Mom serves everyone ramen and hands out plates for the kimbap. "Jal meok-ge-sseum-ni-da!" we say to thank Mom for cooking us dinner.

After we're done eating, we go back to the tent.

Mom, Grandma, Shelly, and I sit underneath it. Ray

stands in front of us to perform his dance. At first, his

back is to us. Then the music begins to play. It's the same K-pop song we've been hearing every day for the last few weeks. As soon as it starts, Ray jumps around to face us. He dances to the beat. As the song speeds up, Ray does a cool spin on his knees. I'm so amazed that I start clapping along to the music. We all do. It almost feels like we're at a concert.

"Woo-hoo!" I shout. "Go, Ray!"

My brother's dance moves get fancier and fancier as the song goes on. He ends with another spin. This time, he jumps so both feet lift up off the floor as he turns. He lands right when the music stops.

"Great job, Ray," Shelly says.

"Thanks, Noona," he says.

"I'm sorry I said your dancing isn't as important as school," Shelly adds. "You're really talented."

I've never seen my brother smile so big.

Mom and Grandma tell him they think he would have won first place. Ray's cheeks turn a little pink, but he's still smiling. I think we were the best audience.

Suddenly, Shelly gets up to look out the living room window. Even from the tent, I can see the rain is still pouring down.

"Is everything okay, Shelly?" Mom asks her.

Shelly sighs. "I was just thinking how I'd be at Professor Ashford's talk on colleges right now."

I was so excited about our camping adventure and watching Ray's dance performance, I almost forgot that Shelly's plans also got cancelled. I feel bad, because even though a field trip to hear about school stuff doesn't sound fun to me, I know it was important to her.

"I'm sorry, honey," Mom says. "Is there something we can do?"

Shelly shakes her head. But I have an idea. I dig through the pillows and blankets until I find my bag of camping supplies. I grab the bag and flip it over. Everything falls out.

"What are you doing?" Ray asks me.

"I have a very good reason for this," I tell everyone because I know that this might look like a mess. It's not, though. I have a plan. I find what I'm looking for: my notebook.

I turn to Mom and ask very sweetly, "Mom, can we borrow your laptop?"

This time, Mom says yes right away. "I don't know what you're up to, Olive, but I trust you."

"Thanks, Umma."

"I'll go get it," she says. While we wait, Ray looks through my camping supplies.

"Slime!" he shouts. "I love slime."

"Me too," I say. "That's why I packed it."

"What else is in here?" Ray looks at each item from my bag, including my *Handbook of Constellations*.

I give my notebook to Shelly.

"What's this for?" she asks.

"Since you didn't get to go on your field trip, you could write down your own observations about colleges."

"Okay," Shelly says. "Where do I start?" She opens my notebook to a blank page. Mom comes back with her laptop just in time. We turn it on.

"First, you can look up a school you're interested in and write down important information you find. Next, you could list the school's special features. Then, you could write down if you think you would like that school or not."

Shelly's face lights up. "Olive, where did you get this idea? It's terrific."

"At school," I say. "Mrs. Bramble taught us how to be like scientists and write down our observations about flowers and plants. I thought maybe you could do the same with colleges. But I also got the idea from you. You taught me how to make lists. I know it's not the same as a professor helping you, but it could be a start."

"I could put the information I find in a spreadsheet to compare and contrast," Shelly says excitedly. "Olive, you are the smartest, sweetest sister ever."

"I am?" I ask.

Shelly nods.

"What about me?" Ray asks both of us.

My sister and I laugh. "You are the coolest, funniest brother ever!" I say.

The three of us are laughing when Mom says, "Okay, time to wash up for bed."

"Yes, Umma," we all say. One by one, we take turns brushing our teeth. I don't even complain that I am the last one to finish. I don't want this day to end!

By the time I'm back from the bathroom, everybody is in the tent under the blankets.

Mom yawns. I do too. Shelly and Grandma close their eyes.

"Hey, Olive?" Ray says sleepily.

"Yeah?"

"Thanks for making me come out of my room. This day turned out better than I expected."

"Yes, for me too," Shelly adds.

Suddenly, Ray jumps out of the tent. "I almost forgot!"

"What is it?" I ask.

"Shelly and I have a surprise for you," Ray says. "Since you couldn't go see the stars, we brought them to you." Then my brother turns off all the lights.

Our house gets dark, and I notice something glowing above me. Stars! Ray found my glow-in-the-dark stars for emergencies! He and Shelly stuck the stars on the bedsheet so we can see them when we are lying down. And they included all my favorite constellations: Cassiopeia, the Big Dipper, the Little Dipper, and Leo.

"Shelly and Ray, you are the best siblings ever!" I shout. I give each of them a big hug.

Mom, Grandma, Shelly, and Ray laugh even though I broke the inside-voice rule. Oops. Right now, I'm too happy to be quiet. The rain outside seems to agree, because it starts pouring even harder. I don't mind, though, because I love rain. Even though none of our plans worked out, I'm glad we got to spend the day together.

Chapter 10

In the morning, I wake up bright and early. Shelly and Ray are still sleeping. But Grandma is already in her wheelchair in front of the window. Quietly, I get out of our tent and join her.

I remember that mornings are *not* for shouting, so I whisper, "Good morning, Halmoni."

"Good morning, Olive," she whispers back. "Look outside."

I take a look, and guess what? No more rain. And

best of all, there is a rainbow in the sky! Mr. Garcia is already outside, walking his puppy.

"It stopped raining," I say.

Grandma puts her arm around my waist. "Your mom and I know you were disappointed about the camping trip with your friends. But you were able to make this weekend very special for our family, so we have a surprise for you."

"A surprise?"

Grandma looks out the window. "There they are."

Right then, Mr. Wong's car pulls up in our driveway.

"Marcus is here?!" I shout, forgetting all about being quiet. Behind me, Shelly and Ray wake up. Oops.

"I'm sorry, everyone, but I have a very important guest," I say. Then I hurry to put on my rain boots and blue hat, even though there is no rain. I really like this rainy-day look. It might even be my new favorite outfit.

I rush out the door right as Marcus gets out of the car. I'm running over to give him a high five when more people come out of the car. The Wongs brought Cory with them! And Greta too!

"This is the best surprise ever," I say.

I'm so excited that I start jumping up and down, splashing water from a puddle. My friends join me, and we all jump and splash together. Then I bring them inside to show them my tent.

"Wow," Greta says. "Olive, this is wonderful!"

"Is that banana milk?" Marcus asks me. I look inside the tent. Shelly and Ray are gone. Instead, I see a tray of Korean snacks and four banana-milk cartons. It's all the snacks I chose from the market.

Mom pokes her head out of the hallway to say hello to everyone. She must have put the snacks in the tent while I was outside. "A camping trip is not complete without snacks. Right, Olive?"

"Right." I give Mom two thumbs up.

My friends and I sit down under the tent and dig in.

"These snacks are awesome," Cory says. "Especially this one." He holds up a chip shaped like a whale.

"I love those too," Greta adds.

After we're done eating, Marcus says, "I brought the observations on my mom's new flowers. Want to see?"

"Yeah," I say.

"Me too," Greta says.

"Me three," Cory adds.

Marcus takes out a small notebook from his pocket. He opens it up and shows us pages filled with drawings of flowers and notes.

"You're like a real scientist, Marcus," I say. "And those are really good drawings. It feels like we really did go outdoors to see nature."

"You're right," Cory agrees. "Very good *observation!*"

Greta and I laugh.

I'm so glad my friends are here.

Then I remember the best part. I get up to close the curtains of the living room window so that our house is dark.

"What are you doing, Olive?" Cory asks.

"I'm going to bring even more of the outdoors indoors," I say. I grab my bag and pull out my *Handbook of Constellations*. Then I lie down inside the tent. "Look."

My friends lie down too. We all look up at the glow-in-the-dark stars my brother and sister stuck to the bedsheet.

"If we study the patterns of stars, we can be

astronomers," I tell my friends. I show them my handbook, and we use it to find the stars on the sheet.

"Cool," Greta says, searching through the book for the constellation in front of her.

"I can't wait to tell Mrs. Bramble what we did this weekend," Marcus says.

Greta and Cory nod with smiles on their faces.

I smile biggest of all. "We went camping under the stars."

The End

Discussion Questions

1. Have you ever had to change or cancel your plans because of the weather? What did you choose to do instead?

2. At the start of the story, Olive and her siblings don't get along. But by the end, they're able to work together. What changed?

3. Olive plans activities to help her brother and sister cheer up. How would you encourage someone who was feeling disappointed?

4. Olive and her siblings have very different plans for the weekend. If you were making plans for a really great weekend, what would you choose to do?

About the Author

Tina Kim spent her childhood dreaming of becoming an artist one day. Somehow she ended up writing about artists instead—and she loves every minute of it. When she is not writing, Tina likes to eat lots of mac and cheese and watch travel documentaries with her dog, Henry. She lives in Los Angeles, California.

About the Illustrator

Tiff Bartel is a multimedia artist, creating work in illustration, design, film, and music. She lives in Winnipeg, Manitoba, Canada with her husband and baby, and their cat and dog.

31901068435686